Happy

Birthday

Love,

Glenda

WISH YOU WERE HERE!

Happy New Year from Michaella

this is me

I missed you for so long
Please write

I Send lots of kisses

HAPPY

HAPPY

Fadders

Day

meow

to yous.

COUSIN Beth

thank you for the present.

Please I need a visit soon.

I squished a bug

P.S.

by mistake.

x x x x x x x

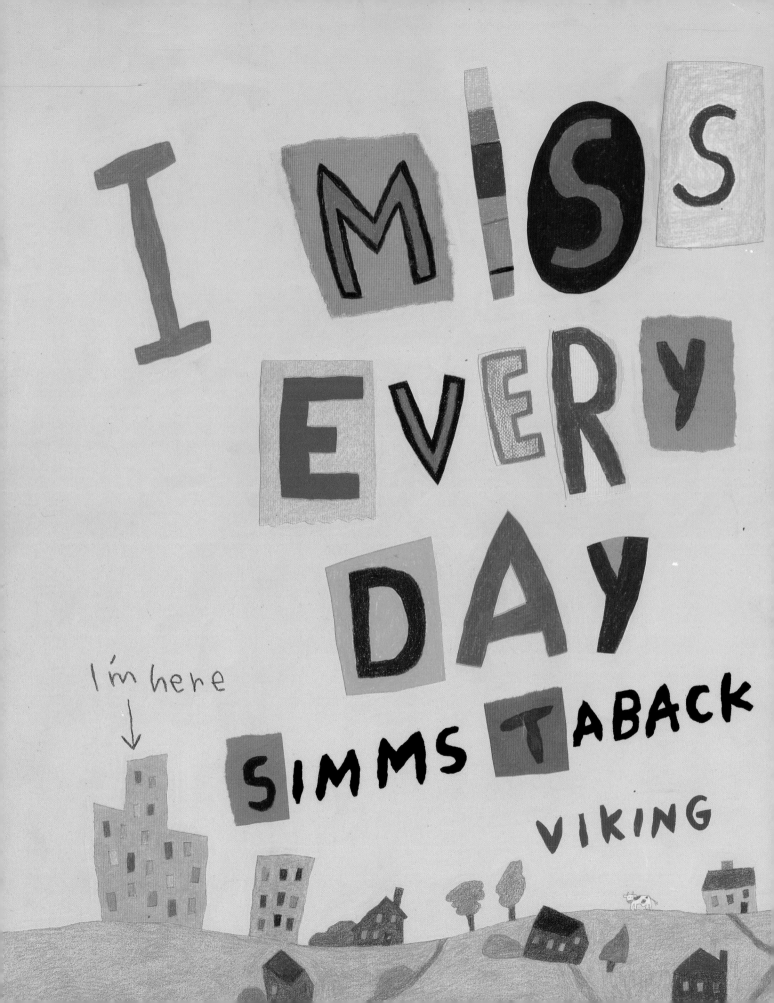

or when it's wet and gray

I think about you all the time

I'm going to wrap myself just like a present

I'll paint it bright and gay

I'll tie it with my favorite ribbon

I'm going to jump inside a nice big box

I'll write your address on the front

I miss you every day

I'll jump into a mailbag

I'll climb into your mailbox

You will find me in the mailbox

There's some postage yet to pay

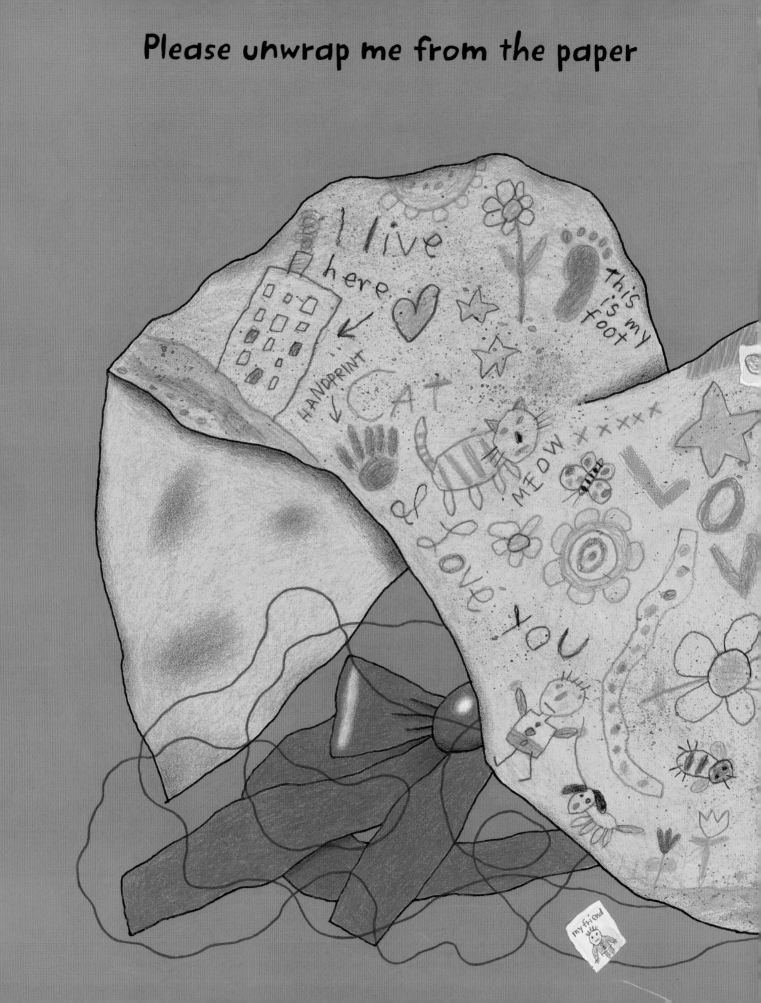

Tuck me in and read a story

and everything will be O.K.

I miss you so much.

A Birthday cake for you.

Happy Holiday

Roses are red, violets are blue, I would love to visit you. goodest your friend, Oliver

Grandpa and Grandma So how old are you?

Dedicated to Sophie
U.S. 3¢

See you soon!

How are you? I am good. your friend,

Simon

Miss you once, miss you twice Because you are Very nice.

FROM KATE

Nelson is a friend of mine. He can visit ANYtime!

Thanks to Woody Guthrie, whose song inspired this book

VIKING
Published by Penguin Group
Penguin Young Readers Group, 345 Hudson Street, New York, New York 10014, U.S.A.
Penguin Group (Canada), 90 Eglinton Avenue East, Suite 700, Toronto,
Ontario, Canada M4P 2Y3 (a division of Pearson Penguin Canada Inc.)

Penguin Books Ltd, Registered Offices: 80 Strand, London WC2R ORL, England

First published in 2007 by Viking, a division of Penguin Young Readers Group

1 3 5 7 9 10 8 6 4 2

Copyright © Simms Taback, 2007
All rights reserved

LIBRARY OF CONGRESS CATALOGING-IN-PUBLICATION DATA
Taback, Simms.
I miss you every day / by Simms Taback.
p. cm.
Summary: A little girl misses someone so much that she wraps
herself up like a package and sends herself through the mail.
ISBN 978-0-670-06192-1 (hardcover)
[1. Postal service—Fiction. 2. Stories in rhyme.] I. Title.
PZ8.3.T1145Ia 2007   [E]—dc22   2007008046

Manufactured in China